BURNING
OF THE
BIG TOP

Margaret Scariano

A **HIGH ADVENTURE** BOOK
High Noon Books
Novato, California

Cover Design: Jim McConnell
Interior Illustrations: Herb Heidinger

International Standard Book Number: 0-87879-407-7

10 09 08 07 06 05 04
15 14 13 12

High Noon Books
a division of ATP
20 Commercial Blvd.
Novato, California 94949

Contents

Chapter 1

Clown for a Day

Sometimes Jed Fields felt like punching Harv Huxley out. Like right now. Jed picked up the evening newspaper on the seat beside him. He shoved the coffee cup to one side. "Harv, you're always against trying anything new. Where's your spirit of adventure?" he asked.

"Aw, come off it, Jed. I don't want a job with the circus. I know it's only to help them set up. Only one day. But I'm a city boy. I don't want anything to do with tents or wild animals. Mr. West's enough of a wild animal for me."

Jed laughed. He and Harv worked as beginning mechanics at West's Garage. "One day's work, Harv. That's all. You want extra money to buy that speed boat. This is your chance. Just listen. I'll read the ad to you."

He opened the newspaper to the help wanted ads. He read, "Wanted: strong workers to set up

1

circus tents. Apply at fairgrounds ticket booth. 8:00 A.M., July 10."

Harv laughed and pounded the table with his fist. "Jed, Jed." He shook his head. "They want *strong* men. Why, I bet you don't weigh 120 pounds dripping wet! A good puff of wind would blow you away." He laughed again.

Jed gritted his teeth. Most of the time Harv was a good buddy. But sometimes he bugged him with his big body talk. Like being six foot three made Harv closer to heaven. "Well, muscle man, how about it?" Jed asked.

"All right. I'll go with you. But just to help set up the tents. Nothing to do with the wild animals. No way!"

The next morning they stood in line at the ticket booth. It didn't look much like a circus yet. But still Jed felt the excitement. Men and women hurried about. He watched them put up their booths. Lots of ways to win prizes, he thought. Other people were getting their stands ready. All kinds of stands—hot dogs, cotton candy, cold drinks, apples on a stick, popcorn, and tacos.

He saw a huge canvas tent lying on the ground. It would be used for the three-ring circus. Ropes lay on the edge of the canvas. There were several long poles lying nearby.

Jed could hear a band playing. He watched a man tossing straw from a truck. Another man with a rake spread the straw on the ground. And the smells! Dust and animals and excitement. Jed hoped the jobs wouldn't be filled before Harv and he got a chance.

Finally, Harv was next in line. The man hiring took one look at Harv's size. "You're hired. Report to the man standing by the red and yellow umbrella," he said.

"How about my buddy here?" Harv asked. He pointed to Jed.

The man looked up. He shook his head. "Sorry. He's not big enough. We need muscle to set up the circus. Next."

"Come on, Jed. I didn't want to work for the circus anyway." Harv started to walk toward the car.

"You work, Harv. It's all right." Jed tried to sound cheerful. But it hurt not even to be given a chance. "See you tonight."

"Hey, fella. Looking for work?" A man in clown's make-up stood in front of Jed.

"Yeah, but guess they want bigger guys," Jed said. He started to walk away.

"Hey, wait, man. Maybe our act can use you. My brother's got the flu. I need someone to take his place. You could do it easy. You're the right size."

Every nerve in Jed's body tingled with excitement. "Me?"

"Sure. Wouldn't you like to be clown for a day?"

Chapter 2

Fun and Sweat

"Hey. You. The big guy." The man by the red and yellow umbrella yelled, "You going to work or clown around?"

"Guess he means me," Harv said. "See you at the hot dog stand for lunch, Jed." Jed watched him hurry over to the man.

The clown asked, "Well, is it a deal? Will you fill in for my brother?"

"Sure. And my name's Jed. Jed Fields."

"Follow me, Jed. I'm Clancy, the clown. I'll show you what we do. It's not hard. The main thing is to have fun. Then the audience has fun too. We'll pick up a costume for you at my trailer."

Jed walked to the trailer with Clancy. At the trailer door he turned and looked back. Harv had his shirt off. He was pounding in iron spikes with a sledge hammer. Other men were setting up the poles. "They're going to have that tent up fast," Jed said to Clancy.

"Yep. They know what they're doing." Inside the trailer Clancy sat Jed down in front of a large mirror. "I'll tell you what you'll be doing. Mainly, it's being my partner. You'll do practically everything I do—like twins. Doing what I do is part of the humor. But, first, we have to get you a face." Clancy opened a drawer. It was filled with jars and brushes. "Let's see. Maybe I could do something different with eye make-up."

"I think *you* look great," Jed said. "Why don't you make me up like you?"

"Oh, no, Jed. My made-up face is my trademark. Every clown invents his own face. No one copies another's make-up. It's the code of the circus." Clancy took the top off of a jar and handed it to Jed. "Here. This is the basic white paint for your face. Start with this."

Then Clancy tried different lines around Jed's eyes. He decided to outline Jed's eyes in a diamond-shape. He drew a wide smile on Jed's face. "Now for the costume. Baggy pants, checked jacket, big, floppy shoes, and a straw hat." Clancy tossed the clothes on the chair. "Get into these. After you put on the clothes, you'll really feel like a clown."

"Every clown invents his own face."

Jed dressed. He looked in the mirror. He didn't look like himself at all. Even Harv wouldn't know him! He laughed at himself in the mirror. But then he thought about the clown act. What was he supposed to do? And all those people in the stands would be watching him. His mouth was so dry, he could barely swallow. And his heart began to pound.

"Maybe this isn't such a good idea, Clancy. I may look like a clown but I'm not sure I can act like one."

Clancy laughed. "Don't worry. We'll just run through the act a few times. I'll cover for you if you make a mistake."

For the next two hours Clancy showed Jed how to be a clown. They tripped over ropes. They bumped into each other. They squirted water from water pistols at each other. They practiced a trick with the other clowns. The trick was to crowd a lot of clowns into one small car. And then drive it into the center ring of the circus. The audience loved to see fifteen clowns get out of the tiny car.

"It's lunch time, Jed." Clancy patted him on his back. "Meet me at the trailer at 12:45. You did all right this morning, Bozo!"

Jed walked toward the hot dog stand. He was hungry. Clowning was hard work. And Harv would really be surprised at how he looked.

Harv was waiting for him. He slumped in a folding chair. His face was sweaty and covered with dirt.

"Hi, guy," Jed said in a clown-voice.

"Bug off. I'm waiting for a friend." Then Harv

added, "At least I *thought* we were friends. Until he got me into this mess."

Harv sat up straight. He looked closely at Jed. "It *is* you. I didn't know you." Then he slumped back in his chair. "And, to tell you the truth, I'm sure sorry I do."

"What's wrong, Harv?" Jed asked.

"I'll tell you what's wrong. I let you talk me into this job. That's what's wrong." Harv looked hot and angry.

"You're just hungry. I'll get us some hot dogs. You'll feel better then, Harv."

Harv and Jed ate their hot dogs. At first they were too hungry to talk. Then Jed told Harv about Clancy and the tricks they had practiced.

"Want to hear about my morning?" Harv tossed his paper plate in the trash bin. "Most of the morning I pounded iron spikes. They hold the tent to the ground."

"That wasn't hard for you, Harv. You're strong," Jed said.

"I was doing all right. Then some guy dropped his sledge hammer on my foot." Harv pulled off his shoe. His foot was black and blue.

"Then what happened?" Jed asked.

"While I was sitting on the ground holding my foot, a man bent down. He asked me what was wrong. I looked up. It was the snake man. And, Jed, he had the biggest snake I've ever seen hanging around his neck."

"Gosh! What did you do?" Jed didn't like snakes any better than Harv did.

"I yelled. The snake slid off the man's neck. It went right over my leg. The man finally caught it. It was hiding under a pile of newspapers."

"That's scary, all right. But the rest of the morning went OK, didn't it?" Jed asked.

"Oh, sure." Harv frowned. "We were ready to raise the big top. It's all done by ropes, you know. Well, the foreman forgot to tell me when to let go." He held out his hands. The rope burns on them were bright red.

Jed looked at his watch. "Hey, I gotta go. Clancy said to meet him at 12:45."

"Go ahead. I'm going to call it a day. Might go bowling."

"Don't go now, Harv. Stick around for the afternoon show. I'm what they call the run-in clown. That's the guy who comes into the ring while they change the act and get the props. Props. That's what they call things they use in an act. I do funny things. I trip over the ring. I try to climb a rope and slip. I lift heavy bar bells."

"You? Lift bar bells? If you're so strong, why

weren't you pounding spikes with me this morning? Oh—I get it. The bar bells are fake. Right? They just look like they weigh a lot. But they're probably rubber or plastic or something. You really had me going there for a minute, Jed." Harv laughed. "Yeah, that's real funny. A little guy like you acting like a strong man. Maybe I will catch your act."

Chapter 3

Jed's First Trick

Jed hurried toward Clancy's trailer. Poor Harv. He always expected to win, be the best, because he was so big and strong. He'd had a rough morning, Jed thought. And somehow his big size hadn't helped him.

Jed knocked on the trailer door. No answer. Then he opened the door, stuck his head in, and called, "Clancy, I'm back."

"Clancy told me to tell you to go on in. He's fixing some soup for his brother," a man said. "He'll be back in a few minutes."

Jed turned and looked at the man. He tried not to stare. "Oh—thanks. Thanks very much," he said. Jed stepped inside the trailer. He couldn't help peeking out the window at the man. He was covered from head to toe with tattoos. He had hearts on his arms. A dragon seemed to snort smoke on his back. Across his chest the word "mother" was tattooed in red ink. His legs were tattooed with snakes that wound around and around from his ankles to his knees. As the man walked away, the snakes seemed to be slithering up his legs.

Jed was glad to see Clancy coming. Clancy wasted no time. "First thing is to check your make-up, Jed. Then be sure you have all the props for the act." Clancy laughed. "One time my brother pulled a water pistol from his pocket. He aimed and pulled the trigger. Nothing. No water and no laughs either. So check all your props."

"All right, Clancy. I'll fill this water pistol right now," Jed said.

Clancy looked at his watch. "Fifteen minutes until the afternoon show. I'm going to check on my brother. See if he needs anything. I'll meet you just before circus time where the performers go into the big tent." Clancy slapped Jack on the back. "Don't worry. You'll do fine."

Jed checked his make-up. He filled his water pistol and tucked it in his pants pocket. He looked in the mirror again. The audience should laugh just looking at him.

Then he heard a yell. He guessed the circus people were tense, too. But now it was a scream.

A scream filled with fear. Someone needed help. Jed dashed to the door. He stopped. What if the snake were loose again? He was scared of snakes. He couldn't help it. Now he heard another scream. It was louder. Whoever was screaming was really scared! Jed threw open the door.

The first thing he saw was the fat lady. She stood between Clancy's trailer and the animal cages. A huge tiger walked around her. Now and then his big tongue licked his mouth. His jagged teeth gleamed in the sunlight. Even from the trailer Jed could see his yellow eyes watching the fat lady. The tiger walked around and around. Then he stopped. He crouched down. Waiting. Ready to pounce.

Now the fat lady had stopped screaming. Jed could hear her sobs.

Sweat broke out on Jed's forehead. Chills raced down his back. His feet felt glued to the floor. He could almost smell the fat lady's fear. Jed gulped. He couldn't just stand there and let the tiger attack.

He took a deep breath and slowly moved down the trailer steps. No way did he want to surprise that tiger! He saw the animal trainer. He had a bucket of fresh meat in one hand. In the other hand he carried a long pole with a hook on the end. The trainer tried to get the tiger's attention. He dangled the fresh meat and called softly, "Here, Duke. Got a treat for you. Come on, Duke."

But Duke kept his eye on the fat lady. Jed slowly stepped in front of the fat lady. The tiger's tail switched back and forth. He opened his mouth wide. A low growl came out.

Every nerve in Jed's body was tense. His mouth was dry. And his legs were shaking. He looked at the trainer. In a whisper he said, "Move closer to me. When I say 'meat,' hold out your pole with a chunk of meat on the end."

The tiger took a step. His tail switched back and forth. He didn't look friendly—not at all like a dog wagging his tail. Then the tiger raised his head and roared. The sound sent shivers up and down Jed's back. But he didn't move. In a way he felt as if he were all alone. No trainer. No fat lady. No circus performers. Just him and the tiger staring at each other. Waiting.

The tiger took a step toward him. Then another. Jed's heart pounded. The tiger crouched in an attack position.

"Meat!" Jed yelled. At the same time he pulled out his water pistol and aimed. The stream of water hit the tiger in the nose. He shook his huge head. He blinked his eyes.

The trainer held out the pole with the meat on the end. The tiger sniffed. He stood up. He shook his head again. Then he followed the trainer and the meat into his cage.

The fat lady threw her arms around Jed. He felt a rib crack. Other circus people slapped him

*At the same time he pulled out
the water pistol and aimed.*

16

on the back. "Good job, clown."

Jed thought nothing would ever scare him that much again. The circus music began. Everyone hurried off to get ready for the opening parade.

Jed stood beside the trailer. He heard the audience clapping. "Come on, Jed. This is it," Clancy called from the tent entrance.

Frozen fear gripped Jed. All those people were going to be watching *him*! It would almost be easier to face the tiger again.

Chapter 4

Jed Enters the Ring

Clancy stood by the elephant. "Come on, Jed. I'll show you how to get on."

"Me?" Jed looked up at the animal. Even its legs were taller than he. Someone brought a ladder and placed it against the elephant.

"Up you go, clown." Clancy held the ladder.

Jed felt as if he were climbing a huge, grey mountain. Finally he sat on top of the elephant. He looked down. How far it looked to the ground!

Clancy took the ladder away. The trainer tapped the elephant's leg. They were moving! Jed sat on the bright cloth on the back of the elephant. There were straps to hold onto. At first, he gripped the straps tightly. With each step Jed was sure he would slip off. But then he began to get used to the roll of the elephant's walk. He no longer had to hold onto the straps so tightly.

Jed rode by the tiger's cage. The trainer was sitting on a barrel at the end of the cage. He was smoking. Guess he wasn't taking any chances. He wasn't going to let that tiger escape again. Jed wondered how the tiger had got out. Had someone left the cage unlocked? Or did the tiger slip out when the trainer was feeding him? Oh, well, it really didn't matter. The fat lady didn't get hurt. But I sure was scared, Jed thought.

They went into the big tent. The elephant stopped. "Come on, Sophie," the trainer yelled to Jed's elephant. "The band's playing your song." The band blared out with a marching song. Sophie stepped high just as if she were marching.

Jed heard the crowd yell and clap. Sophie seemed to know what to do. She followed the elephant in front of her. Around the track they went. The grand parade. Horses, dogs, elephants, caged lions and tigers, and clowns. The fat lady rode on the flat bed of a truck. The truck was covered with red, white, and blue streamers. The bearded lady and the toothpick girl rode on the truck with the fat lady. The toothpick girl was really thin! The strong man was showing his muscles. He wore only leopard-skin shorts. Then there was the tallest man in the world. Jed thought he must be eight feet high. The tall man stood next to the midget. The top of the midget's head barely reached the tall man's knee. Now that's what I should do, Jed thought. I should stand next to a midget. Then I'd look big, too.

Jed looked back at the circus acts behind Sophie and him. What a view! Jed could see it all from his high seat on the elephant. It was great seeing all the circus sights. He forgot to be scared about being part of the circus. People in the audience whistled and shouted.

He wondered where Harv was sitting. Then he saw him. Just behind two rows of kids from the town's youth camp. The kids were eating popcorn and cotton candy. They were all dressed in yellow t-shirts with a big bear on the front. Even the adult with them wore a yellow t-shirt. Sophie walked in front of them. Jed called out. "Hi, Harv. Up here!" Harv looked his way. Jed waved. Harv waved, too. But as if he were waving at a stranger. Jed laughed. Harv didn't know him in his clown get-up! For some reason it made Jed feel powerful. Like he was hidden or something.

Jed saw the ringmaster step inside the center ring. He looked neat with his high black boots. Except for the boots he was dressed all in white.

Even his top hat was white. He blew a whistle. Like magic, the acrobats in the end rings started doing cartwheels.

The grand parade was over. Sophie knew what to do. She walked over to the elephant trainer. He helped Jed down.

"Thanks for the ride, Sophie." Jed patted her trunk.

"Better go over to where the clowns enter the ring," the trainer said. "Your act is coming up soon."

Jed stood by the entrance. He watched the high-wire act. The acrobats flew through the air like birds. Several times Jed was sure they were going to fall. Each time it was part of the act. They would miss the first swinging bar on purpose and then catch the next one. Jed's heart stopped each time it happened.

The ringmaster blew his whistle. I'm on next, Jed thought. His palms felt sweaty. Clancy ran by on his way to the center ring. "Come on, Jed. Do your stuff."

Jed took a deep breath. He ran after Clancy. The crowd went wild. They cheered and clapped. When Clancy fell over trying to step into the center ring, the audience laughed.

At first Jed felt silly and stiff. He was glad for

the clown make-up. He could hide behind it.

Clancy set up a card table with some dishes and three chairs. He waved to Jed to sit down on one of the chairs. Just then another clown drove a small car into the center ring. The ringmaster said over the loud speaker, "Looks like Clancy and his friend have a visitor. It's a good thing there are three chairs."

Clancy made a sign to Jed to open the car door. Jed bowed. He turned the door handle. It spun around. Jed walked to the other door. But it had no handle. Jed looked over at Clancy and shrugged. The crowd laughed. And suddenly Jed didn't feel foolish anymore. It was fun making people laugh.

Then Clancy came over to the car. He tried the handle, too. It didn't work for him either. Then he waved to the clown inside the car to crawl out the window.

First, the driver climbed out. Jed and Clancy helped him. But then another clown popped his head out the window. And another. And another. There were fifteen clowns in that tiny car! The audience whistled and yelled for more.

Then Clancy pointed to the high-wires. He poked his chest and pointed to the rim around the circus ring. He stepped upon the rim. With his arms straight out he balanced himself. Even Jed laughed. Clancy acting like he was on a high-wire was funny. Then Clancy pointed to Jed to walk the rim.

Jed remembered what they had practiced that morning. Carefully he placed his feet in the huge shoes on the rim. No way could he walk on it. Clancy pretended to be angry. Jed tried again. When Clancy wasn't looking, Jed put one foot on each side of the rim.

Clancy turned and saw Jed's trick. He chased him. Now the other clowns had made a human tunnel with their legs spread apart. Jed dashed into the tunnel with Clancy right behind him. Clancy almost caught Jed. But Jed broke through the tunnel. The ringmaster blew his whistle. Jed ran from the center ring with Clancy right on his heels. Just before Jed left the ring, he turned and squirted Clancy with the water pistol.

Outside the tent Clancy shook Jed's hand. "You did great, Jed. You have the makings of a fine clown."

Jed wanted to see the next act. He watched some men lower a large steel cage over the center ring.

The ringmaster said, "Ladies and gentlemen. They're man-eating. They're dangerous. They're hungry. Meet Leo Limpski and his trained tigers!"

Jed wondered if Duke was one of the tigers. He didn't care if the tigers were trained or not. He was just glad there was a cage around them.

Chapter 5

Signal for Disaster

Jed watched the trainer, Mr. Limpski, with his trained tigers. Jed couldn't believe it. Mr. Limpski opened the cage doors and let six huge tigers out. He cracked his long black whip over his head. The tigers jumped up on high stools. All except one tiger. He walked round and round his stool. Every once in a while, he stopped and growled. Mr. Limpski snapped the whip. Still the tiger padded round and round the stool. Jed bet that tiger's name was Duke. Mr. Limpski cracked the whip once again. This time it was close to the tiger. And this time he jumped up on his stool.

Mr. Limpski placed three large hoops across from the tigers. Each hoop was wrapped with burnable material. Mr. Limpski lit the hoops. They made a ring of fire. With another snap of his whip Mr. Limpski sent the tigers leaping through the flaming hoops. The audience clapped and cheered.

Mr. Limpski then made the tigers do the hardest trick of all. The three biggest tigers lined up side by side. The next two tigers jumped on their backs. Finally the sixth tiger leaped up to stand on top of them all.

Now the trainer had the animals march around in a circle. Each tiger held the tail of the tiger in front of him in his mouth.

Suddenly Jed heard a crackling sound. Like a dozen whips snapping the air. Jed looked at Mr. Limpski. He hadn't snapped his whip. He looked at the other two rings. Men were getting them ready for an act with horses. But no one was cracking a whip. Then Jed smelled it. Smoke!

He looked up at the audience. Was someone smoking inside the big tent? It was against the law. But he didn't see anyone smoking. Jed turned and looked at the opening in the tent where all the acts came in. Billows of black smoke curled around the entrance.

He dashed outside. The straw which had been spread around the animal cages was on fire. The smell of the burning straw gagged him. His eyes stung from the smoke. He had to warn the people in the big tent. He began to run into the tent and then stopped suddenly. No way could he rush in there and yell "Fire!" That would really cause a panic. Maybe he could put the fire out himself.

He rushed back to the animal cages. The fire had spread. Instead of just smoking straw, now there were places where flames blazed.

Jed saw a bucket by Duke's cage. He remembered seeing a water faucet next to Clancy's trailer. He filled the bucket and ran back to the burning straw. He dumped the water and tore back to the faucet. After his third trip to the faucet, Jed knew he had to have help to put out the fire. It was spreading fast. Already the ground around Duke's cage was burned black. The fire was heading toward the big tent.

Jed dropped the bucket and hurried to the big tent. The horses were dancing to the band's music. The ringmaster was standing just outside the center ring. He was watching a famous high-wire family near the top of the tent.

Jed dashed up to the ringmaster. "Sir, sir." He tugged at the man's sleeve.

The ringmaster looked down at Jed. He frowned. "Not *now,* clown. You come on right after the Wild West show."

"I need help. There's a fire by the tigers' cages.

I tried to put it out. But it's spreading."

The ringmaster acted as if he hadn't heard Jed. In a low voice he said, "Quick. Tell the band leader to play *The Stars and Stripes Forever.*"

What was wrong with this guy anyway? He acted as if the show must go on even with a fire. "Don't you understand? I said fire!"

The ring master gave Jed a little shove. "I understand. Now go! Quick. To the band leader *Stars and Stripes Forever* is a circus signal for disaster."

Chapter 6

Clowns to the Rescue

Jed ran to the bandstand. He yelled up at the band leader. But the leader only smiled and nodded. He must think I'm clowning around, Jed thought. I've got to get near the band. He jumped from bench to bench. He squeezed past people. Once he lost his balance and almost sat on a lady's lap.

The people thought he was part of a clown act. "Is that your real face, man?" a little boy asked. He pulled on Jed's coat sleeve.

"Yeah. Sure." Jed jerked loose. He kept climbing from bench to bench. Up, up. He had to reach the band leader. And quick! In his mind he saw the fire coming closer to the big tent. At least he couldn't see any smoke yet.

Finally he got to the bandstand. He dodged between the trumpets and the trombones. At last he was almost to the leader.

He stopped a moment. He didn't want to yell "Fire!" at the conductor. Should he wait until the music stopped? Then he remembered what the ringmaster had said.

Jed rushed up to the band leader. "The ringmaster said to play *The Stars and Stripes Forever.*"

The band leader looked at Jed. Then he looked down at the ringmaster. But he never missed a beat. With a wave of his baton he ended the music. He tapped his music stand. *"Stars and Stripes Forever,"* he said to the band. At once the band began to play the lively music.

"Get back to center ring, clown. You'll be needed there," the band leader said.

Jed couldn't believe how easily the band had switched to the disaster music. It was just as if it were part of the program.

Quickly he made his way back down through the stands. People were still cheering and clapping. Jed was glad they didn't know that disaster burned just a few hundred yards from them.

He heard the whistle of the ringmaster. He saw the high-wire acrobats begin to climb down. The horses in the outside rings trotted around once. Then they leaped over the rim and left the tent. Elephants pulled the tiger cages out of the big tent. It all seemed so calm.

"Hey, Jed. Follow me." Clancy shouted. He led the way into the center ring. Other clowns joined them. They turned somersaults, squirted each other with water pistols, and juggled.

The clowns all seemed to know what to do. Jed copied what they did. He didn't want to look over to where he'd spotted the smoke. Still it was hard not to.

"Hey, Jed, stand here," Clancy shouted. Jed ran to the center of the ring. "Kneel down. We're going to do a trick. Don't worry if you can't support my weight. It's funnier if you fall on your belly."

Jed couldn't help asking. "What about the fire? Is it out?"

Clancy put one foot on Jed's back. He took it off. Then he put his hands on Jed's back and tried to climb on. He rolled off and lay next to Jed. "I can't see the smoke from here, Jed, but don't worry. Circus people know how to handle such things." He stood up. The audience whistled and cheered. Finally Clancy stood on Jed's back, and Jed collapsed.

From the corner of his eye Jed saw the first tiny flames at the side wall of the tent. So far no one in the audience seemed aware of the danger.

Elephants pulled the tiger cages out of the big tent.

Would the ringmaster tell them? Maybe the ground crew already had the fire under control.

The large truck with the red, white and blue streamers drove into the tent. A clown was driving it. He stopped in front of the section with the children from the town's youth camp. He jumped out of the truck. He quickly walked over to the child sitting at the end of the bench. He took her hand in his. He gave a signal to the other children to follow him. Another clown helped load the children and their leader on the truck bed. The kids were laughing. The crowd clapped. They must have thought it was a special treat, Jed thought. He saw Harv clapping and laughing, too. When all of the children were on the truck, the clown drove it around the circus ring and out the exit.

Then the ringmaster stepped into the center ring. He blew his whistle. Jed followed Clancy to the rim of the ring. The ringmaster said, "Ladies and gentlemen, it will be necessary to leave the big tent. There is a fire."

Someone screamed. Then another. And another.

"Please. Please. There is no need to panic. Our ground people are putting out the fire. But to be safe, we ask you to calmly leave your seats. Walk outside."

"Fire! Fire!" someone yelled. And the crowd began to pile out of the stands. It was a mass of screaming, shoving, shouting people. All trying to escape.

"Let's go!" Clancy shouted to the clowns. "Jake, you try to lead the people from the west section. Willie, take the east. Bobby, try to calm the south section. And, Eric, you're in charge of the north. Go, clowns."

"Hey, Clancy. What about me?" Jed asked.

"Do what you can to help people," Clancy said.

Jed turned to see where he might help. Then a thought came to him. Harv! Where was Harv?

Chapter 7

Jed's Old Trick

Jed climbed up on the rim of the ring. He had to find Harv. Harv had been sitting just above the kids from the town's youth camp. He wasn't there now. Maybe he was already out. People were crowding around the main exit.

Jed smelled smoke now. Small flames began to show at the opening in the top of the tent. People were screaming. For a moment he saw Clancy. He was helping an old man with a cane. But there were hundreds of people ahead of them. They'll never make it, Jed thought. There were just too many people trying to get out at one time.

Jed rubbed his burning eyes. The smoke was really getting to them. There must be another way to get some of the people out. Then he remembered something. When he was a kid, he and his friends used to sneak under the flaps of the circus tent. If a person could sneak in, why couldn't he sneak out?

Jed jumped off the rim and ran to one side of the tent. He crawled underneath the stands to the tent. He jerked on the edge of it. It didn't budge. A little farther down Jed jerked again. The tent flap seemed to give a little. Jed kicked at it to loosen it more. Finally he loosened it enough so a child could crawl under. A grown-up would have to squeeze a little bit. But maybe it would loosen more as it was used.

Jed ran to the people trying to get out. He yelled at a woman. She held two children by their hands. They were crying.

"Hey, lady. Follow me. I think you can squeeze out under the flap."

She looked at him like he was a crazy clown. She shook her head. She tried to shove through the crowd ahead of her.

"Listen to me, lady." Jed grabbed her arm. "Follow me. I'll get you and your kids out under the flap." Jed bent down and picked up one of the children. "Come on." The woman and the other child followed Jed to the loose tent flap.

He set the child on the ground. "What's your name, son?" he asked.

"Timmy."

"Well, Timmy, I'm going to show you a secret

way out. When you are on the outside, wait for your mom. OK?"

Timmy had stopped crying. "Is she going to come out a secret way, too?"

"Yes." Jed told Timmy to get on his belly. He lifted the flap up as high as he could. "Now wiggle under, Timmy."

Timmy crawled under the tent flap like a little worm. Finally he was on the outside.

"You next," Jed said to the woman.

"I can't get under that. I'm too big." The woman looked around wildly. "Shove Sue through. Maybe I can get through the crowd if I don't have the kids."

"No way. Get down and squeeze through." Jed ordered. "Hurry. I've got to help some others."

The woman crawled. She wiggled. She pushed her way under the flap. Then Jed shoved the little girl through.

"Thanks. Oh, thank you, clown." The woman cried. "Come on, kids. Let's get out of here."

Jed ran back to the crowd. Again and again he helped people crawl under the flap of the tent.

Most of the people crawled through quickly and easily. Jed didn't even look closely at them. He held the flap and yelled at the people to hurry up. His voice was hoarse from the yelling and the smoke. He'd held the flap up so long, his arm felt as if it were going to drop off. Twin girls were next in line. But Jed didn't know whether they'd make it or not. They were identical twins right down to the last pound. And that was the problem! The girls were too big around to crawl through.

"You're going to have to really squeeze," Jed said. "One go through and the other push. Then when the next one goes through, the one on the outside can pull. Pushing or pulling is your only chance."

When the second twin popped through the opening, Jed sighed with relief and turned to see who else needed help.

On his fourth trip to the crowd he spotted Harv near the band stand. But the band wasn't playing anymore. Harv's face was streaked with dirt and blood.

"Harv, are you all right? It's me. Jed."

Harv looked at him. But he didn't act as if he knew who Jed was. Then Jed saw the bump on Harv's forehead. Someone or something had hit him.

Jed took his hand. "Come on, Harv. Let's get out of here." Jed led Harv and several other people to the loose flap. First, he helped the children crawl under. Then the grown-ups.

Harv just stood there. He didn't seem to know what was going on. Jed looked over at the people still trying to get out of the tent. Was there time to help a few more? The tent was dark with smoke. There was a crackling sound. Jed looked up. One of the poles that held up the tent was on

Harv took out his knife and began to slash the tent.

fire. One end of the tent was burning. If he hurried, maybe a few more people could be saved. Did he dare leave Harv here alone? And how was Harv ever going to squeeze under that small opening? Jed didn't know, but he had to try.

"You're next, Harv." Jed pointed to the small opening. "Crawl under. Come on."

Harv looked at Jed. He shook his head. He reached in his pocket and took out his knife and began to slash the tent. Then he kicked the weak canvas with his foot and crawled through.

Jed sighed with relief. Now he could help more people get out.

Again and again Jed led people to the opening. He could barely see across the ring because of the thick, black smoke. He had just shoved an old man and his grandson under the flap when he heard the noise. It sounded like a bad wind storm. The big top seemed to groan.

Chapter 8

Headlines!

Now Jed saw flames and thick smoke everywhere. He knew he had to work fast. He dashed across the ring and ran around the burning center pole. Again and again he led people to safety.

By now the smoke was so thick he could see only a few feet. Was everyone out? He couldn't see or hear anyone else. Then he heard a loud crack. It must be the center pole, Jed thought. He scrambled through the opening. The big top collapsed with a rush of hot air.

"That's the clown! That's the guy," someone shouted.

Jed sank down to the ground. He coughed. His eyes and nose burned from the smoke.

"Yeah. He saved our lives." The woman with the two children pointed at Jed.

"I thought you were a goner, man." Harv bent

over and pounded him on the back.

Jed sat up. "You're all right?" he asked.

"Sure. I was dazed. Something fell and hit me on the head." Harv pounded Jed on the back again. "But you, old buddy, you saved my life. And lots of other people, too."

A newspaper reporter with a camera walked up to Jed. "What's your name?" he asked.

After Jed gave his name, the reporter asked many questions. Jed told about the brave clowns. "They kept on with their act in center ring even though they knew there was a fire." Jed paused and then added. "And they're the ones who drove the kids from the youth camp to safety '

Out of the corner of his eye he saw Clancy on a stretcher. Jed broke away from the reporter. He hurried to catch up with the paramedics who were carrying Clancy.

"Clancy!" Jed called.

Clancy's leg was in a splint. He turned his head and looked at Jed. "Hi there, kid. Glad you made it." Tears ran down his face. His white clown make-up was streaked and dirty.

"What happened to your leg?" Jed asked.

"One of the tent poles fell on it. But I'll be back in center ring in no time."

"Good for you." Jed took his hand and shook it.

The paramedics started for the ambulance. Clancy yelled out, "Hey, kid, if you ever want a job with the circus, I could sure use a gutsy guy—and a natural born clown. You did all right."

The next day was Sunday. Jed and Harv sat in the coffee shop. Harv said, "Look at this. You made the headlines."

Jed read the headline, **"Good Things Come In Small Packages."** It made him feel funny. He wished Harv would cool it. But Harv stopped everyone who walked by the booth. "Did you read about my buddy, Jed Fields? He's a hero. A real hero." Then he'd read from the newspaper article.

By now Jed knew the article by heart. It read, "Jed Fields—small in height but big in courage—helped dozens of people out of the circus big top to safety." Then it went on and on about the part-time job as a clown because he was too small to get a job setting up the circus. The article praised Jed, a little guy, for his big act of bravery.

Jed reached for another piece of toast. It was funny, he thought. He'd always felt small. As

Harv said, "Look at this. You made the headlines."

long as he could remember, his friends were bigger and stronger. And being small always had bothered him a little. Made him feel less important than his buddies. He sat back and grinned. It would never, never bother him again.